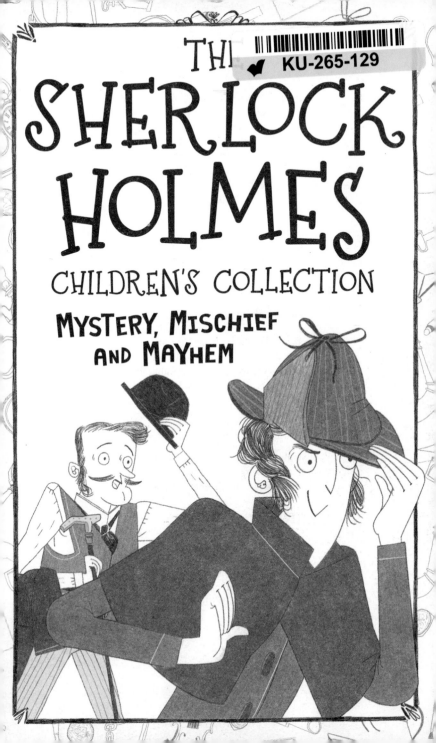

KU-265-129

THE SHERLOCK HOLMES

CHILDREN'S COLLECTION

MYSTERY, MISCHIEF AND MAYHEM

Published by Sweet Cherry Publishing Limited
Unit 36, Vulcan House,
Vulcan Road,
Leicester, LE5 3EF
United Kingdom

First published in the UK in 2020
2020 edition

2 4 6 8 10 9 7 5 3 1

ISBN: 978-1-78226-420-0

© Sweet Cherry Publishing

Sherlock Holmes: A Scandal in Bohemia

Based on the original story from Sir Arthur Conan Doyle,
adapted by Stephanie Baudet.
Cover design by Arianna Bellucci and Rhiannon Izard
Illustrations by Arianna Bellucci

www.sweetcherrypublishing.com

Printed and bound in China
C.WM004

SHERLOCK HOLMES

A SCANDAL IN BOHEMIA

SIR ARTHUR CONAN DOYLE

Sherlock Holmes is certainly not like other men. He is a thinking and observing machine. He has no time for other people. He is not interested in friendships (except for ours, I would like to think) and he would certainly not waste his time on any type of romantic relationship.

I know that he thinks of some women as pretty – he has told me so, himself. But I have never seen him give more than two minutes of his attention to any woman. Well, except for one. The one he calls *the* woman.

Her name is Irene Adler.

One night, towards the end of March, 1888, I happened to be passing Baker Street on my way home from visiting a patient.

I hadn't seen my friend, Sherlock Holmes, for some time. My medical practice took up most of my time, and I devoted the rest to my dear wife.

Every now
and then the
newspapers
would tell me
a little about what
Holmes was doing. He
still liked to study crime
and use his extraordinary
powers to solve the
mysteries that baffled the police.

In the case of the Trepoff
murder he had been sent to
Odessa, a city in Ukraine. He had
also cleared up the tragedy of the
Atkinson brothers in Ceylon. And

after that he had carefully carried
out a mission for the royal family
of Holland.

Besides these stories, I knew
nothing of my friend's day-to-day
activities.

It was raining on that day
in late March, and there were
not many cabs free. As I passed
the well-remembered door, I
looked up to Holmes' window
and suddenly wanted to see him
again. His rooms were brightly
lit, and I saw the silhouette of his
tall, slim figure pass twice behind

the blind. He was walking briskly up and down the room with his head sunk on his chest and his hands clasped behind him. This was a walk I had seen many times  before. It meant that Holmes was at work. He was clearly hot on the scent of some new mystery.

I rang the bell.

It was answered by the landlady, Mrs Hudson.

'Oh, Doctor Watson, sir. You're soaking wet! Let me have your coat! This damp will not do your war wound any good.'

I smiled at her and took off my wet things.

'Mr Holmes is in one of his moods. He doesn't want me to send dinner up until he calls,'

she tutted. 'But I am sure he will
be pleased to see *you*.' house mate

I climbed the stairs to the
rooms that I used to rent with
Holmes and knocked on the door.

He did not seem very pleased
to see me at first, but I knew
that he was just distracted by his
problem. Deep down I knew that
he was glad I was there. There
was a friendly look in his eye as
he waved me to an armchair and
offered me a cigar. Then he stood
by the fire and looked at me in his
strange, thoughtful way.

'Marriage suits you,' he said. 'I think, Watson, that you have put on seven and a half pounds since I saw you.'

'Seven,' I answered.

'Just a little more I think, Watson. And I understand that you have your own doctor's surgery now? You did not tell *me* that you planned to buy a practice.'

'Then how do you know?' I wasn't surprised that he knew, but his way of working things out always interested me.

'I see it. I deduce it. How do I know that you have been getting yourself very wet lately? And that you have a most clumsy and careless servant girl?'

'My dear Holmes,' I said. 'This is too much. You would have been burned as a witch if you had lived a few centuries ago. I was caught in the rain just now, of course. And I suffered the same fate on Thursday. I took a country walk and came home in a dreadful mess. But I can't imagine how you deduced that. As to Mary Jane,

13

the maid, she is hopeless and my wife has asked her to leave. But again, I fail to see how you worked it out.'

Holmes chuckled to himself and rubbed his long, thin hands together. I smiled as I waited for his reply. He loved to show off his talents, especially to me.

'Simple,' he said. 'I can see that on the inside of your right shoe the leather has six parallel cuts. These were caused by someone very carelessly scraping around the sole to remove dried mud.

A double deduction, you see. I can tell that you have been in bad weather and that your servant is a careless cleaner.'

I nodded, lifting up my right foot to check that what he said was right.

'Now to your medical practice,' he continued. 'Picture this: a man walks into my room smelling of antiseptic. He also has a bulge on the right-hand pocket of his waistcoat, where he hides his stethoscope. Can I deduce that he is anything else but a doctor?'

I laughed. 'When you explain it, it always seems so simple,' I said. 'I often think I should be able to do it myself, yet I never manage it. I'm sure my eyes are as good as yours, though.'

'Yes.' He looked at me with

that small, smug smirk I knew so well. Then he flung himself into an armchair. 'You *see* but you do not *observe.* The difference is clear. For example, you have often climbed the stairs from the hall to this room, haven't you?'

'Of course.'

'How often?'

'It must be hundreds of times,' I said.

'Then how many stairs are there?'

I frowned. 'I have never counted them. I have no idea.'

'Exactly. You have seen but not observed. That is my point. I know that there are seventeen steps because I have seen *and* observed.'

I had to admit that he was right. Though I could not think of a time when I would ever need to know how many stairs there were at 221B Baker Street.

'By the way,' Holmes went on. 'As you are still interested in these little mysteries, you may be interested in this.' He threw over a sheet of thick, pink-tinted note paper that had been lying open on the table. 'It came by post this morning. Read it aloud.'

The note was undated and without any signature or address.

At quarter to eight o'clock tonight, a gentleman will call. He would like your help with something very important. Your recent work with one of the royal families of Europe has shown that you can be trusted with very important matters. Please be in your rooms at that time. Do not think it odd if your visitor wears a mask.

'This is certainly a mystery,' I said. 'What do you think it means?'

'I have no information yet. It is a big mistake to guess the answer before you have the facts, Watson. It is so easy to twist the clues to suit the theories instead of finding theories to suit the facts. But the note itself. What do you deduce from it?'

He was testing me again. I knew he enjoyed these little tests as much as I did.

I looked closely at the note again and examined both the writing and the paper.

'The man who wrote it is quite rich,' I began, trying to imitate my friend's ways. 'This paper could not be bought cheaply. Quite the opposite. It is unusually strong and stiff.'

'Unusually – that is the very word,' said Holmes. 'It is not an English paper at all. Hold it up to the light.'

I did so and saw the letters Eg, P and Gt woven into the texture of the paper.'

'What do you make of that?' asked Holmes.

'The name of the maker, no doubt. Or it could be the initials of the man who wrote the letter.'

Holmes shook his head.

'Not at all. The Gt stands for *Gesellschaft,* which is German for company. P, of course, stands for *papier.* Now for the Eg. Let us glance at our *Continental Gazetteer.*'

22

He took down a heavy, brown book from a shelf.

'Eglow, Eglonitz – here we are, Egria. It is in a German-speaking country in Bohemia, not far from Carlsbad.

'"Egria is known for its many glass factories and paper mills,"' he read.

Then he looked up at me. 'Ha ha, my boy, now what do you think of that?' His eyes sparkled and

Continental Gazetteer

An extremely useful book. The Continental Gazetteer is a sort of geographical dictionary that gives information on every country in the world, from A to Z. Knowing even just a little about a country can be useful in a case.

brought a smile to my face too. His
boyish enthusiasm was catching.

'The paper was made in
Bohemia,' I said.

'Exactly! And the man who
wrote the note is German. We can
tell from the way he has written
this sentence,' Holmes explained,
pointing to the note. 'You see: "At
quarter to eight o'clock tonight
a gentleman will call." The verb
is at the end of the sentence. No
Frenchman or Russian would
have written this.'

I nodded. My knowledge of

German did extend that far.

'All that remains is to find out what is wanted by this man. This German who writes on Bohemian paper and prefers to wear a mask than show his face. Ah, here he comes now, if I am not mistaken.'

As he spoke, I could hear the sound of horses' hooves coming to a stop outside. Carriage wheels grated against the kerb, and the doorbell suffered a sharp tug.

'A pair of horses, by the sound of it,' Holmes said. He walked over

Curb

to the window and
peered down into
the street below.
'Yes, a nice little
carriage and a pair of
beautiful matching grey
horses. A hundred

main hero
sidekick

Coins

and fifty guineas each I would
guess. There's money in this case,
Watson, if there is nothing else.'

'I think I had better go, Holmes,'
I said, getting up from my chair.

'No, Watson. Stay where you
are. I am lost without my loyal
sidekick. This looks as though it
will be interesting. It would be a
pity to miss it.'

'But your client ...'

'Never mind him. I may want
your help and so may he. Here he
comes. Sit down again, and give
us your best attention.'

We heard some voices in the hall. I recognised Mrs Hudson's excited tones. She was always keen to meet new visitors.

Slow, heavy footsteps made their way up the stairs and along the passage. The steps stopped right outside the door. Next came a loud and firm knock.

'Come in!' said Holmes.

The man who entered was very tall, with a huge chest and powerful limbs like Hercules. Anyone in England would think that his rich clothes were

Greek
mythology

strange, but he wore them well.
Heavy bands of silky brown fur
decorated the sleeves and front
of his double-breasted coat. A
deep blue cloak was thrown
over his shoulders and hung like
water down his back. It was lined
with flame-red silk and fastened
at the neck with a magnificent
red crystal brooch. His boots
came halfway up his calves
and were trimmed at the top
with rich brown fur. His whole
appearance gave the impression
of luxury.

Neither Holmes nor I could speak for a moment as we gazed at this man. We had never seen anyone like him before.

Across the upper part of his face he wore a black mask, which he had just been putting in place as he came in.

'You had my note?' he asked in a strong German accent. His deep, booming voice broke the silence of the room. 'I told you that I would call.' He looked from one to the other of us, not sure who to talk to.

'Please take a seat,' said Holmes. 'This is my friend and colleague, Doctor Watson. He is kind enough to help me with my cases. May I ask who you are?'

'You may address me as the Count von Kramm, a Bohemian nobleman. I hope that this gentleman, your friend, is a man of honour. I must be able to trust him with a very important matter. If not, I will need to talk to you alone.'

I got up to go but Holmes caught me by the wrist and pushed me back into my chair.

'It is both or none,' he said. 'Anything you say to me can be said in front of Doctor Watson.'

The count shrugged his broad shoulders. 'Then I must begin,' he said, 'by binding you to absolute secrecy for two years. At the end of that time the matter will no longer be important. At present it is so vital that it could change European history.'

'I promise,' said Holmes.

'And I,' I said.

'You will excuse this mask,' continued our strange visitor.

'My noble employer wants my identity to remain a secret. I admit that even the name I have just given you is not my own.'

'I know,' said Holmes, dryly.

'You see, Mr Holmes, we are at risk of a huge scandal. If the details of the matter were to get out, they could harm one of the royal families of Europe,' he said. Then he bent his head down and peered about the room as if looking for eyes in the walls. 'I speak of the great House of Ormstein, hereditary kings of Bohemia,' he whispered.

'I knew that also,' said Holmes.

I listened to Holmes with astonishment – I could not fathom how he knew all this.

Holmes settled down in his armchair and closed his eyes. Our visitor stared in utter shock at the relaxed figure, unsure whether to continue his speech.

The short silence made Holmes open his eyes and look impatiently at his huge client. 'If Your Majesty would be good enough to tell us the story, I would be able to advise you better.'

The man sprang from his chair and paced up and down the room. He looked equally surprised and angry. Suddenly he paused, tore the mask from his face and hurled it to the floor.

'You are right!' he cried.

'I am the king. Why should I try to hide it?'

I gasped, but Holmes just leaned forwards a little.

'Why, indeed,' he murmured. 'Before Your Majesty had even spoken I knew who you were.

I am talking to Wilhelm
Gottsreich Sigismond von
Ormstein, Grand Duke of Cassel-
Felstein and King of Bohemia.'

'I am not used to doing such
business as this myself,' said our
visitor. He sat down once more
and passed his hand over his high
white forehead. 'Yet the matter
is so delicate that I could not
confide in anyone else. So I have
travelled over from Prague to
consult you directly.'

'Then please consult,' said
Holmes, closing his eyes once

more. I was a little embarrassed at his rudeness considering that he was speaking to a king.

'The facts are these. Some five years ago, during a long visit to Warsaw, I met a well-known singer called Irene Adler. I expect you know the name?'

'Please look her up in my index, Watson' murmured Holmes, without opening his eyes.

For many years Holmes had collected articles on all kinds of things. His collection was huge now, and spoke of every imaginable person and subject. I found Irene Adler's information nestled between that of a Hebrew rabbi and the author of an article on deep-sea fishing.

'Let me see,' said Holmes. He reached for the scrapbook and began reading aloud.

Miss Irene Adler, singer

Born in New Jersey, USA, in 1858.
A singer – contralto.
La Scala Opera House, Milan.
Prima donna, Imperial Opera of Warsaw.
Retired from the operatic stage.
Living in London.

Master of the Seas, John
Williams is best known for his

'Hmm – quite so! Your Majesty, as I understand, got to know this lady well. You wrote her some very personal letters and would now like to get them back.'

'Exactly, but how …'

'Was there a secret marriage?'

'No.'

'No legal papers or certificates?'

'No.'

'Then I fail to see your problem. Even if this young person tried to use these letters to blackmail you, how is she to prove that they are genuine?'

'They are written in my handwriting,' said the king.

'Pooh! Forgery!'

'On my private notepaper.'

'Stolen.'

'With my own wax seal.'

Holmes waved his hand.
'Copied'

'She has my photograph.'

'Bought.'

'We were both in the photograph.'

Holmes sighed and I looked at him a moment. I had enjoyed this quick-fire conversation. Holmes had an answer for everything, but so did the king. It had been a duel of words and I could almost hear the clash of the swords.

'Oh dear,' said Holmes. 'That is very bad! Your Majesty has indeed acted foolishly.'

'I was mad – insane. I was only a prince then. I was young. I am only thirty now.'

'We must get the photograph back,' said Holmes.

The king shrugged. 'We have tried and failed.'

'Your Majesty must pay. It must be bought.'

'She will not sell.'

'Steal it then.'

The king shook his head. 'We have tried five times. Twice I have paid burglars to search her house. Once we stole her luggage when she was travelling. And twice she has been stopped and searched in her carriage. We still could not find it.'

'There was no sign of it at all?' Holmes asked, a little shocked.

'Absolutely none.' The king uttered. I could see a certain sad hopelessness brewing behind his eyes. I felt sorry for him. We all do foolish things when we are young, but we never expect them to come back to haunt us in later years.

'It's quite a problem,' said Holmes with a laugh.

'But a very serious one to me,' said the king, looking annoyed.

'Very serious indeed,' Holmes replied, still smirking slightly. 'And what does she plan to do with the photograph?'

'To ruin me.'

'But how?'

'I am about to be married.'

'So I have heard.'

It was news to me. But, of course, Holmes knew – he was always one step ahead of the conversation.

'To Clothilde Lothman von Saxe-Meningen, second daughter of the king of Scandinavia. Her family is extremely strict and she is extremely sensitive. If she found out about the relationship between myself and Irene, the engagement would be over.'

'Does Miss Adler plan to tell them?'

'She threatens to send them the photograph of us. And she will do it. I know that she will do it. You do not know her, but she has a soul of steel. She has the most beautiful face I have ever seen, but behind it lies a stubborn mind. She is desperately in love with me, and she would do anything to stop me from marrying another woman.'

'Are you sure that she has not sent it yet?'

'I am sure.'

'And why?'

'Because she has said that she will send it on the day our engagement is announced. That will be next Monday.'

'Ah, then we have three days left,' said Holmes with a yawn. 'That is very lucky, because I have one or two important matters to look into first.'

I gasped at his cheek, but should not have been surprised. Holmes had probably unravelled the whole mystery in his head.

And it was just like him to show little respect to royalty – he does not care for people's titles. To Holmes, a client is a client, royal or not.

I glanced at the king, who was looking at Holmes with a mixture of shock and hopelessness. I could see that he did not expect this story to end well.

'Your Majesty will, of course, stay in London for a while?'

'Certainly. You will find me at the Langham Hotel, under the name of the Count von Kremm.'

decoy

'Then I shall write to let you know how we progress in the case.'

'Please do so. I shall be waiting anxiously.'

'And – as to money?'

'Take however much you like. There is no budget or limit.'

'Absolutely no limit?'

'I would give one of the provinces of my kingdom to have that photograph.'

'And for present expenses?'

The king took a heavy leather bag from under his cloak and laid it on the table. 'Here is three

hundred pounds in gold and
seven hundred pounds in notes,'
he said. 'Will that be enough?'

Holmes nodded, scribbled a
receipt on a sheet of his notebook
and handed it to the king. 'And
the lady's address?' he said.

'Briony Lodge, Serpentine Avenue, St John's Wood.'

Holmes made a note of it. 'Then, good night, your majesty. I am sure we will have some good news for you very soon.'

The moment we heard the wheels of the royal carriage rolling down the street, Holmes picked up the money with glee. 'Come, Watson. We can have dinner at Romano's tonight.'

Later, after a wonderful meal, we went our separate ways. I travelled home, while Holmes

set off to St James' Hall to see
Tchaikovsky conducting his
music. That was obviously one of
the 'other important matters' that
he had mentioned to the king.

'Please call at Baker Street at
three o'clock tomorrow afternoon,
Watson. We will discuss the case
then,' said Holmes, with a wave of
his hand.

At three o'clock
exactly the following
afternoon I rang the
doorbell of number
221B Baker Street.

'Mr Holmes is not back yet,' Mrs Hudson told me, opening the door to let me enter. 'He left the house just after eight o'clock this morning.'

I went upstairs into the sitting room and settled myself in a comfortable chair by the fire. There I sat and waited for Holmes to return. The minutes ticked past slowly, but I was in no rush to leave. I was fascinated by this strange case and keen to hear how Holmes would unravel the mystery.

It was nearly four o'clock when the door opened and a shabby-looking man with side whiskers walked into the room. He was red-faced and wearing ragged and dirty clothes.

By now I was used to my friend's amazing talent for disguises. Yet, I still had to look three times before I was certain that it was indeed Holmes. He stumbled through the sitting room to his bedroom, tearing off his wig as he went. Just five minutes later, he reappeared wearing a tweed suit and looking as smart as ever.

Holmes looked at me and then slumped into an armchair. He stretched out his legs in front of him and laughed heartily.

'It's so funny, Watson,' he said, almost choking on his laughter.

'What is?'

'I am sure you could never guess how I have spent the morning.'

'No, I can't imagine,' I said with a smile. 'I suppose you have been closely watching Miss Irene Adler.'

'Yes, I was. But what happened later was quite unusual. Let me tell you. I left the house just after eight o'clock this morning dressed as an out-of-work horse groom.'

Mrs Hudson never told me about Holmes' disguise. But then again, she was so used to his strange habits that having a muck-covered horse groom walking through the hall would not have seemed strange at all.

'I soon found Briony Lodge,' he went on. 'It's a quaint little villa, with a garden at the back but

none at the front. On the right side of the house there's a large, well-furnished sitting room. It has long windows that stretch almost to the floor and those silly English window fasteners that a child could open.

'After I had examined every detail of the house, I took a stroll down the street. There, I found the exact people I was hoping to meet: a small group of cabmen tending to their horses. I tell you, Watson, that men who work with horses are just the friendliest bunch. I lent them a hand and was paid in money, sandwiches and as much information as I could want about Miss Adler. They also told me about half a dozen other people in the neighbourhood that I had no interest in at all. But, I had to listen just the same.'

I smiled as I pictured Holmes trying not to look bored. I hoped the side whiskers hid his frown.

'What did you hear about Irene Adler?' I asked.

'Oh, all the men in Serpentine Avenue admire her. She is the prettiest person in the whole village, they all say. She lives quietly, sings at concerts, drives out at five o'clock every day and returns at seven sharp for dinner. She rarely goes out at other times except to sing.

'She has only one male visitor, but he comes often – at least once a day. He is dark and handsome, they say. His name is Mr Godfrey Norton. He is a very respected lawyer'

'A lawyer,' I said, noting the fact in my mind.

Holmes nodded. 'You see how useful it is to become friendly with cabmen, Watson? The men had driven him home many times from Serpentine Avenue. They knew all about him. When I had listened to all they had to tell,

I started to think of a plan.

'This Godfrey Norton was important in the case. The fact that he was a lawyer was worrying. Why did he visit Irene so often? What was the relationship between them? Were they in love or was he helping her to blackmail the king? Would she have given him the photograph? Should I continue my work at Briony Lodge or search Norton's office?

'I'm afraid I am boring you with these details, Watson. But you must know all the little problems

I face if you are going to help me solve the big one.'

'I am following you closely. Please continue,' I said.

'Well, I was still concocting my plan when a cab drove up to Briony Lodge. A very handsome man – dark, with a straight nose and a moustache – jumped out of it. This was the man I'd been told about: Godfrey Norton.

He seemed to be in a great hurry. He shouted to the cabman to wait for him, ran up to the door and rushed past the maid as soon as she opened it.

'He was in the house about half an hour. I caught glimpses of him in the windows of the sitting room. He was pacing up and down, talking excitedly and waving his arms. I could see nothing of Irene Adler, however. At last he came out, looking more flustered than before. As he stepped up to the cab he pulled a gold watch from his

pocket and looked at it. Another
spark of panic flashed across
his face. "Drive like the devil!"
he shouted. "First to Gross and
Hankey's in Regent Street, and
then to the Church of St Monica
in Edgeware Road. Half a guinea
if you do it in twenty minutes!"'

'Now, what could he want at
Gross and Hankey's jewellers?'
I mused.

'Patience, Watson! And you
shall see. Well, away he went at
an almighty speed. I was just
wondering whether I should

follow him when up the lane
came another neat little carriage.
It had hardly stopped when Miss
Irene Adler shot out of the front
door and into it. And what a
lovely woman she was. She had a
face that a man might die for.'

I raised my eyebrows. 'It's not like you to talk like that, Holmes.'

He shook his head and tutted. 'It is a metaphor, Watson, nothing else.

'"The Church of St Monica, John," she cried, "and half a sovereign if you reach it in twenty minutes."

'This was too good to lose, Watson. I was wondering whether to run after the carriages, but luckily a cab came down the street just in time. The driver looked twice at picking up such a shabby person as me in my groom's disguise. But I jumped in before he could object.'

'"The Church of St Monica," I said, "and half a sovereign if you reach it in twenty minutes." It was twenty-five minutes to twelve, and of course it was clear to me what was happening.'

It was now clear to me too, but I didn't interrupt Holmes. This was quite a story.

'My cabby drove fast. I don't think I have ever been driven faster, but still the others were there before us. I paid the man

and hurried into the church.
There was not a soul there except
Godfrey Norton, Irene Adler, and
a clergyman, who seemed to be
arguing with them. They were all
standing in a group in front of the
altar. I sat down in a pew at the
side, trying not to be seen.
Suddenly, to my surprise,
the three at the altar
turned around to
look at me. Then
Godfrey Norton
came sprinting
down the aisle.

'"Thank God," he cried. "You'll
do. Come! Come!"

'"What for?" I asked.

'"Come, man, come. We have
only three minutes before the
marriage license runs out – if we
don't get married in that time, we
cannot get married at all!"

'I was half dragged up to
the altar. Then, before I knew
what was happening, I found
myself mumbling answers that
were whispered in my ear and
promising things I knew nothing
about. I was witnessing the

marriage between Irene Adler and Godfrey Norton. It was all done in an instant. Mr Norton then thanked me with a handshake and Miss Adler with a smile. The clergyman simply beamed at me from the front. I have never found myself in such a ridiculous position.

Just the memory of it started me laughing just now.

'It seemed that the clergyman absolutely refused to marry them without a witness. My lucky appearance saved them from having to drag someone in off the street. As they left, the bride gave me a sovereign. "I don't need no tip, madam," I said.

'"Let us call it a little souvenir," she said. So I shall wear it on my watch-chain in memory of the occasion.' Holmes held up the gold coin for me to see.

'This is all very unexpected,' I said. 'What did you do after the wedding?'

'Well, it seemed that my plans were ruined. I had to come up with a new one. At the church door, they separated – Mr Norton went back to work and Miss Adler, well the new Mrs Norton, returned home.'

'"I shall drive out in the park at five o'clock, as usual," she said to him as she stepped into her carriage. I heard no more. They drove away in different directions and I went off to make my own plans.'

'Which are?'

'Some cold beef and a glass of lemonade,' he answered, ringing the bell for Mrs Hudson. 'I have been too busy to think of food today, and I am likely to be even busier this evening. By the way, Watson, I shall want your help.'

'I would be delighted to help.'

'You don't mind breaking the law?'

'Not at all,' I heard myself say.

'Would you risk being arrested?'

'For a good cause.'

'Oh, the cause is excellent!'

'Then I am your man.'

Holmes smiled. 'I was sure that I could rely on you.'

'But what is it you would like me to help with?'

'When Mrs Hudson has brought the dinner I will explain …'

Just then the lady herself knocked and entered, placing a large tray in front of us.

Holmes looked hungrily at the plates of food, like a lion with his prey. 'I must explain the plan while we eat, for we do not have much time. It is nearly five o'clock now. Miss Irene, or Mrs Norton rather, will return from her drive at seven. We must be at Briony Lodge at exactly seven o'clock to meet her.'

'And what then?' I asked, also tucking into the welcome food.

'Leave that to me. I have everything arranged. There is only one thing I must insist on. You must not interfere, no matter what happens. Do you understand?'

'I am not to do anything? Even if you are in trouble?'

'Nothing whatsoever. There may be some nastiness, but please do not join in. It will end with me being taken into the house. Four or five minutes afterwards the sitting room window will open. You are to stand close to that open window.'

'Right.'

'You are to watch me, carefully.'

'Yes.'

'And when I raise my hand, like this, you will throw

into the room what I give you to throw. At the same time you must call out "fire!" Do you follow me?'

'Of course.'

'It is nothing very alarming.' He took a long, cigar-shaped roll from his pocket. 'It's an ordinary plumber's smoke rocket. That is all you have to do. When you

---

Plumber's smoke rocket

A simple but clever device used by plumbers to find leaks in pipes. When lit, the rocket puffs out thick, grey smoke. The smoke will travel through the pipe and then escape through any holes, showing the plumber where the pipe is leaking from. A plumber's smoke rocket can also be very handy for creating a false fire alarm – simply light the rocket and the smoke will fool everyone into believing there is a real fire.

shout "fire" quite a number of people will join in. You must then walk to the end of the street and I will join you there in ten minutes. I hope I have made myself clear?'

I wondered how sure he could be that all these things would happen at the exact right times. Surely a prediction like this was above even his powers. I nodded anyway, and pushed the worry to the back of my mind. 'I am not to involve myself in the scuffle but to get near the open window. Then, at your signal, I will throw in this object and cry "fire".

Then I will wait for you at the
corner of the street.'

'Yes,' Holmes replied.

'Then I understand. You can
rely on me.'

'Excellent,' he said. 'Now, I think
it's almost time to prepare for the
new role I have to play.'

He disappeared
into his bedroom
and returned
in a few minutes in
the character of a
friendly priest.
He wore a broad

black hat, baggy trousers and a white priest's collar. His soft smile and general look of kindness seemed so real that I was almost convinced it really was a priest who stood in front of me.

Holmes had not simply changed his clothes. His expression, his walk and his very soul seemed to vary with every new role he took on. The stage lost a fine actor the day Sherlock Holmes decided to become a detective.

It was ten minutes to seven when we arrived in Serpentine

Avenue. It was already dusk and the lamplighters were busily working to brighten the grey evening. We paced nervously up and down in front of Briony Lodge, waiting for the arrival of Miss Irene Adler. The house was just as I'd pictured it from Holmes' description, but the area seemed different. For a small street, in a quiet neighbourhood, it was surprisingly busy.

There was a group of shabbily dressed men smoking and laughing on a corner. Near them stood a painter, painting a large canvas, and two cabmen chatting with a nurse. There were also several well-dressed young men strolling up and down with cigars in their mouths.

'You see,' said Holmes, as we gazed at the lit windows of Briony House. 'This marriage makes things easier. The photograph becomes a double-edged sword now. Miss Adler would surely not want her new husband to learn about her relationship with the king, just as the king would not want his princess to discover the truth. Now, the question is, where will we find the photograph?'

'Where, indeed?' I asked.

'It is unlikely that she carries it about with her. The king said the photograph was eight inches by six inches, which is far too large to be hidden in a woman's bag. Plus, she knows that the king is capable of having her stopped and searched. He has already tried that twice.'

'Where would she keep it, then?'

'Perhaps her banker or her lawyer has it. It's possible. But

I think it is also unlikely. Why would she hand it over to anyone else?' he asked. 'She could trust herself, but others may be persuaded to reveal the secret. Besides, her plan was to send the photograph on Monday, when the engagement will be announced. So it must be somewhere where she can quickly lay her hands on it. It must be in her own house.'

'But it has been burgled twice,' I said.

Holmes shook his head. 'They did not know where to look.'

'But how will you know where to look?'

'I will not look.'

'What then?' I asked. Holmes could be very annoying at times. He just loved to keep me in suspense.

'I will get her to show me.'

'She will never agree to show you.'

'She will not be able to refuse, dear Watson. But alas I hear the rumble of wheels. Now carry out my orders exactly.'

As he spoke, the bright glow of the sidelights of a carriage came around the bend. As the carriage pulled up, one of the men from the corner dashed forwards to open the door. He was clearly hoping to earn a penny. But he was elbowed away by another man, who wanted to do the same thing.

A fierce quarrel broke out. Suddenly the two cabmen and the painter joined in. The small squabble turned into a revolving circle of flying fists and angry words.

Miss Irene Adler had stepped out of her carriage just as the heated fight was reaching boiling point. Her delicate face looked lost amidst the sea of flushed red cheeks and sweating brows.

Holmes, dressed as a priest, dashed into the crowd to protect the lady. But just as he reached her he let out a shrill cry and fell to the ground. Blood was running down his face in a steady stream.

As he fell, the angry crowd scattered. Just a few kind people who had seen the fight take place helped attend to the injured man.

Irene Adler hurried up the steps to her house, but paused in her porch. Her fine figure was outlined against the lights of the hall, as she looked back into the street. Her maid, who had opened the door, waited behind her.

'Is the poor gentleman badly hurt?' Irene asked.

'He is dead,' cried several voices.

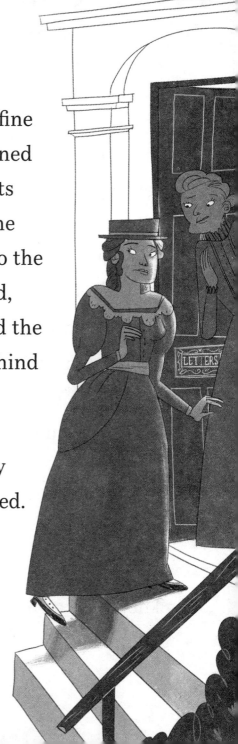

'No, no! There's life in him!' shouted another. 'But he'll be gone before you can get him to hospital.'

I was tempted to run to Holmes and help. Was this all part of his plan or had he really been injured? I took a deep breath and steadied myself, reminding my worried mind that Holmes had insisted I did not interfere.

'He's a brave fellow,' said a woman in the street. 'They would have had the lady's purse and watch if it hadn't been for him. They were a gang, and a rough one too. Ah, he's breathing now.'

'He cannot lie in the road. May we bring him in, madam?'

'Of course. Bring him into the sitting room. There's a comfortable sofa. This way, please.'

Slowly, Holmes was carried into Briony Lodge and laid out in the sitting room. I stayed hidden in the bushes beside the window, watching. The lamps had been lit but the blinds had not been drawn, so I could see Holmes on the couch. He looked weak and badly injured.

I don't know whether Holmes felt any guilt at the way we were fooling this woman, but I did. I have never felt more ashamed in my life than when I saw Irene attend so kindly to Holmes.

And yet I could not fail to complete the plan. Holmes would never forgive me or trust me again. So I hardened my heart and took the smoke rocket out from under my cape. After all, I thought, we were not hurting her. We were stopping her from hurting someone else.

I saw Holmes motion as if he needed air. The maid rushed across and threw open the window. At the same time he raised his hand into the air. This was the moment. I threw the smoke rocket into the room and shouted 'Fire!' as loudly as I could. The words were barely out of my mouth when the

whole crowd joined in. 'Fire!' they cried.

Thick clouds of smoke curled through the room and out of the open window. I caught a glimpse of rushing figures as they fled from the house. Then a moment later, I heard Holmes telling them that it was a false alarm.

Slipping through the noisy crowd, I made my way to the corner of the street. Ten minutes later, I breathed a sigh of relief when I saw Holmes coming down the road to meet me.

We walked swiftly and silently for a few minutes, before turning down one of the quiet streets that lead to Edgeware Road. There we slowed down and paused under a street lamp. There was still a March chill in the air but I was so eager to hear what happened that I did not mind the cold.

'You did very nicely, Watson,' he said. 'Nothing could have been better.'

'You have the photograph?' I asked.

'I know where it is.'

'And how did you find out?'

'Miss Adler showed me, as I told you she would.'

He was being annoyingly mysterious again. I sighed impatiently. 'I am still no wiser.'

'I am not trying to be mysterious,' he said, laughing. 'The idea was perfectly simple. Everyone in the street was paid to help me, you see.'

'I guessed as much,' I replied.

'I asked them to break out into a fight right outside Miss Adler's carriage. Then I approached the scene, as if to save Miss Adler. I made sure to put a little red paint in my hand just before I did so. Then I fell down mid-fight, clapped my hand to my face and smeared the red paint across my forehead. It is an old trick and it worked wonderfully.'

'I guessed that too,' I said. 'Although you acted so well that I admit I was worried for a moment. I thought that you might truly be hurt.'

'I appreciate your worry, Watson. Well, they carried me into the house, as planned. Miss Adler could not refuse helping an injured man of the church, of course. I was taken into the sitting room, as expected, and placed on the sofa. I motioned for air, so they had to open the window, and you had your chance.'

'How did the whole thing help you?' I asked, as we began walking back to Baker Street.

'When a woman thinks her house is on fire, her instinct is

to rush to the one thing that she values most. I thought that, if Miss Adler wanted to blackmail the king, then surely the photograph would be her most precious possession. So naturally she would rush to grab it.

'You really did play your part well, Watson. The smoke and shouting were enough to shake her nerves and send her running for the photograph.

It is hidden in an alcove behind a sliding panel, just above the bell-pull. She was there for only an instant. When I cried out that it was a false alarm, she quickly put the picture back and rushed away. I thought about grabbing the photograph then, but there were too many eyes on me at the time, so I had to leave it.'

'What do we do now, then?' I asked.

'Our quest is almost finished. I shall return to Briony Lodge with the king tomorrow, and with you, if you'd like to come with us. We will be shown into the sitting room to wait for Miss Adler. But, by the time she arrives, neither we nor the photograph will be there.'

'When will you go?'

'At eight o'clock in the morning. She will not be awake yet, so we shall have just enough time to take the photograph and make a quick exit. I will telegraph the king immediately.'

We had reached Baker Street and stopped at the door. Holmes was searching in his pockets for

the key when someone passed
by and said, 'Good night, Mr
Sherlock Holmes.'

The greeting seemed to come
from a slim boy who had hurried by.

'I've heard that
voice before,' said
Holmes, staring down
the dimly lit street.
'I wonder who on
earth that could
have been.'

I had no idea.

Shrugging off the strange event, we stepped inside the familiar halls of 221B.

'Will you stay here tonight?' Holmes asked me, while he hastily scribbled out his telegram to the king. I agreed, and then slyly peeked over his shoulder to see what he had written.

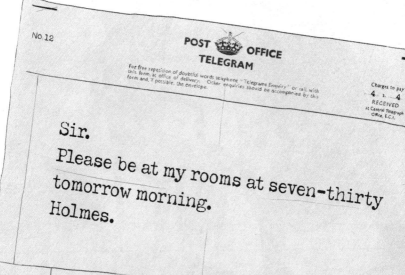

No. 12

POST OFFICE TELEGRAM

For free repetition of doubtful words telephone "Telegram Enquiry" or call, with this form, at office of delivery. Other enquiries should be accompanied by this form and, if possible, the envelope.

Charges to pay
4 s. 4 d
RECEIVED
at Central Telegraph
Office, E.C.1.

Sir.
Please be at my rooms at seven-thirty tomorrow morning.
Holmes.

Office of Origin and Service Instructions or Nature of Ser...
if other than telegram

Lond.

We were in the middle of our toast and coffee the next morning when the King of Bohemia rushed into the room.

'You have really got it!' he cried, grasping Holmes by both shoulders and looking into his face.

'Not yet,' said Holmes, draining his cup. 'But I have hopes.'

'Then, come. I want to sort this now.'

'We need a cab.'

'No, my carriage is waiting,' said the king.

'Then that makes it simpler,' replied Holmes.

We were soon on our way once more to Briony Lodge.

'Irene Adler is married,' remarked Holmes.

'Married! When?' asked the king.

'Yesterday,' Holmes replied.

'Who did she marry?'

'An English lawyer named Norton.'

'But she could not love him,' said the king.

'I hope that she does,' said Holmes.

'Why?' the king asked.

'Because if Miss Adler loves her new husband, she does not love Your Majesty. If she does not love Your Majesty, there is no reason why she should cause any further trouble for you and your marriage plans.'

'It is true. And yet … I wish she had been a princess – an equal to me. Then I could have married her. What a queen she would have made!' He sighed and then fell into a moody silence for the rest of the drive.

When we arrived, we saw that the door of Briony Lodge was already open. An elderly woman stood in the doorway. She watched us step out of the carriage, with a smug smile painted across her wrinkled face.

'Mr Sherlock Holmes, I believe?' she said.

'I am Holmes,' answered my companion. He looked at her in confusion. Holmes had not expected this.

'Mrs Norton said you would probably call. She left this morning with her husband on the five-fifteen train from Charing Cross. They are going to the Continent.'

'What!' Holmes staggered back, his face white with surprise. 'You mean she has left England?'

'Never to return.'

'And the papers?' asked the king, hoarsely. 'All is lost.'

'We shall see.' Holmes pushed past the woman and rushed into the sitting room. The king and I followed. Furniture was scattered about in every direction. Shelves

were dismantled and drawers
hung open, with their contents
scattered across the floor.

Holmes rushed to the bell-pull,
tore back the small sliding shutter
and plunged his hand into the
space behind. He pulled out a
photograph and a letter.

I peered over his shoulder. The
photograph was of Irene Adler
herself, wearing a lovely evening
dress. On the outside of the letter
were the words:

To
Mr Sherlock Holmes.

My friend tore the letter open and held it out so that we could read it together. It was dated midnight of the night before. It read:

Midnight, 24th March 1888

My dear Mr Sherlock Holmes,

You really did very well. You fooled me completely. Right up until the pretend fire, I had no suspicion. But then I realised that I had revealed the photograph's hiding place, and I began to think.

I had been warned against you months ago. I had been told that, if the King employed an agent, it would certainly be you. Even your address had been given to me. Yet, with all this, you still made me show you what you wanted to know. Even after I became suspicious, I found it hard to think badly of such a dear, kind old priest. You truly are very clever. But, you know, I have been trained as an actress myself. I sent John, the coachman, to watch you after the fire. Then I ran upstairs, disguised myself as a young boy, and came down just as you left.

I followed you to your door and heard almost every word of your plans for this morning. Then I rather unwisely wished you good night and walked on to meet my husband.

With you on our tails, we both thought that the best thing to do was to leave immediately. So you will find an empty nest when you call tomorrow.

As to the photograph, your client may rest in peace. I love and am loved by a better man than he. The king may marry whoever he wants. I will not interfere. He treated me very badly. I only keep the photograph to stop him from doing anything with it in the future. But I have left another photograph that he might like to have.

Very truly yours,
Irene Norton, née Adler

'What a woman! Oh, what a woman!' cried the King of Bohemia, when we had all read the letter. 'Didn't I tell you how quick and determined she was? Wouldn't she have made an impressive queen? Isn't it a pity that she was not on my level?'

'She certainly seems to be on a very different level from Your Majesty,' said Holmes, coldly. I hid a smile.

'I am sorry that I have not retrieved your photograph, Your Majesty,' said Holmes.

'Oh nonsense!' cried the king, 'You have done wonderfully well. I know that Irene will keep her word. The photograph is as safe as if it were burnt in the fire.'

'I'm glad to hear you say so.'

'I owe you a lot, Mr Holmes. Please tell me how I can reward you? This ring, perhaps ...' He slipped an emerald snake ring from his finger and held it out in the palm of his hand.

'There is something I would value even more highly,' said Holmes.

'Ask and it shall be yours,' said the king.

'This photograph,' Holmes replied.

The king and I stared at him in amazement.

'Irene's photograph?' he asked. 'Of course, take it, if you wish.'

'Thank you. Then it seems that the case is closed. I wish you a very good morning.' Holmes bowed, ignoring the hand that the king had stretched out to him. Then he stood, walked out the room and out of Briony Lodge forever.

Holmes still speaks of Irene Adler, every now and again. Each time he does, I see his face stretch into a sudden smile.

'I admit it Watson,' he says to me whenever he looks at her photograph. 'She beat me at my own game. I have never come across anyone quite like Irene Adler.'

Sherlock Holmes

World-renowned private detective Sherlock Holmes has solved hundreds of mysteries, and is the author of such fascinating monographs as *Early English Charters* and *The Influence of a Trade Upon the Form of a Hand.* He keeps bees in his free time.

Dr John Watson

Wounded in action at Maiwand, Dr John Watson left the army and moved into 221B Baker Street. There he was surprised to learn that his new friend, Sherlock Holmes, faced daily peril solving crimes, and began documenting his investigations. Dr Watson also runs a doctor's practice.

To download Sherlock Holmes activities, please visit
www.sweetcherrypublishing.com/resources